ISBN 978-0-9954543-1-6
Copyright © 2017 & 2018 Karen Inglis
Published in print by Well Said Press 2018
Published for Kindle/eBook Nov 2017
83 Castelnau, London, SW13 9RT, England

Ferdinand Fox
and the
Hedgehog

by

Karen Inglis

Illustrations by Damir Kundalić

~WS~
Well Said Press

Ferdinand Fox trotted down past the park

where the seesaws and swings stood still in the dark.

His magnificent tail sailed along in the light

of the street lamp above, which lit up the night.

With tongue hanging out and eyes beady sharp,

he trotted on past, heading into the dark.

The path that he took led down to his den,

by a leaning tree with a warbling wren.

That very same night, seeking bugs with her snout,

Hatty the hedgehog was out and about.

As soon as she smelled the scent of a fox

she scampered to hide in an old soggy box.

As she pricked up her prickles and sniffed all around

she saw something move, in front on the ground.

A tiny dark ball scuttled this way and that,

grunting and snorting in satisfied chat.

As the shape moved in closer, with horror, she saw

her tiny son Edmond. He'd slipped out the door!

The scent of the Fox grew stronger and nearer.

She gave a shrill cry, but young Ed didn't hear her.

On turning the bend Ferdinand spied

the playful young Edmond – he'd nowhere to hide!

'**Fox!**' shrieked Edmond. He curled on his side.

Ferdinand froze, his mouth open wide...

'Why, what a sweet hedgehog!' he finally said.

'Why aren't you home, all tucked up in bed?'

Edmond lay shaking, a small prickly ball,

not daring to look, not daring to call.

Ferdinand smiled. 'I'm off now,' he said.

'Don't stay out too late! You should rest your head.'

HEDGEHOG FACTS

Did you know?

A baby hedgehog is called a **HOGLET** ☺

Isn't this one cute?

Hedgehogs can often live for up to **6** or **7** years.

Hedgehog food

Hedgehogs love eating creepy crawlies, like these...!

beetle

caterpillar

snail

earth worms

They also enjoy wet cat or dog pet food – and water.

Hedgehog homes

Hedgehogs make **nests** under piles of leaves and branches, or **inside log piles**, under hedges – or inside compost heaps!

In winter, Hedgehogs have a long sleep called **hibernation**. They usually stay asleep, hidden away, for 12 weeks.

Before going to sleep, they eat lots of insects and autumn fruit, to give them energy over the winter.

Hedgehog spines

A grown-up hedgehog has between 5,000 and 7,000 spines.

If hedgehogs think they are in danger they raise their spines up then roll up into a tight ball!

Helping hedgehogs

Hedgehogs need to walk a long way to find food. We can help them by making small holes under garden fences and walls...

To help them find a place to **hibernate**, we can build up logs, branches and leaves in a quiet part of our garden...

...or we can buy or build a hedgehog house.

Photo credits: Hedgehog Street: Henry Johnson; Trevor Akerman; Alison Taykin | House: wildlifeworld.co.uk
Visit **hedgehogstreet.org.uk** for lots more tips.

FOX FACTS

Foxes are part of the dog family.

A female fox is called a **VIXEN**

A male fox is called a **DOG FOX**

A fox's house is called a **DEN** or **EARTH**

Can you see Ferdinand in his den?

Do you think he's warm and snug in there?

A baby fox is called a **CUB** a **PUP** or a **KIT**

Fox cubs are born blind and deaf and their mother stays with them while their father goes out to hunt for food.

Wild foxes usually live for 1 to 5 years.

(Captive foxes can live for up to **14** years!)

Foxes eat almost anything!

spiders

frogs

mice *(and other wildlife)*

berries

They also love our food ☺

vegetables, meat

bread and sandwiches

FREE COLOUR ILLUSTRATIONS

Visit **kareninglisauthor.com/hedgehog**
to download free fox and hedgehog illustrations to
share with young readers and listeners at story time ☺

Also by Karen Inglis

Ferdinand Fox's Big Sleep (3-5 yrs)

"Ferdinand Fox curled up in the sun, as the church of St Mary struck quarter past one..."

Another gentle rhyming fox tale, based on a true story.

Henry Haynes and the Great Escape (6-8 yrs)

A boy, a bossy boa, a VERY smelly gorilla – and a zoo escape!

Eeek! The Runaway Alien (7-10 yrs) *Laugh-out-loud funny!*

A soccer-mad alien comes to Earth for the World Cup!

Walter Brown and the Magician's Hat (7-10 yrs) *Award winner.*

A magic hat, a talking cat and escaped video monsters...!

The Secret Lake (8-11 yrs) *Karen's best seller. Considered for CBBC TV.*

A lost dog, a hidden time tunnel and secret lake take Stella and Tom to their home and the children living there 100 years ago.

About the author

FB: *facebook.com/kareninglisauthor*   Twitter: *@kareninglis*

Hello! I'm Karen Inglis. I live in London, UK not far from Richmond Park. There are lots of town foxes where I live and my Ferdinand stories are all based on foxes I have seen or heard about from friends. Apart from writing children's books, I love reading, daydreaming, music, theatre — and tea!

Please do leave a review of Ferdinand Fox online if you enjoyed the story – it will mean a lot to me ☺. Thank you!

If you'd like free posters, special offers and new book updates go to **kareninglisauthor.com** to join my **Readers' Club**.

School visits

I love meeting my readers and regularly go into UK schools.

I can also offer **Skype Classroom visits** if you're abroad – or can travel

abroad if budgets allow. If your child's school would like to discuss a visit,

please ask them to email me at kpinglis@wellsaidpress.com.

Find out more at kareninglisauthor.com/school-visits

Acknowledgements

With thanks once again to my illustrator, Damir Kundalić, for bringing another of my Ferdinand Fox stories to life.

And thank you to friends and family who helped with feedback and suggestions to improve the rhyme and rhythm during the early days of writing about Ferdinand Fox and Hatty.

Don't miss…!

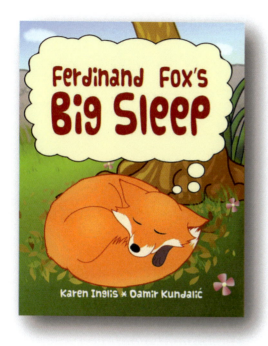

*"Ferdinand Fox curled up in the sun
as the church of St Mary struck quarter past one.
His tummy was full, he was ready for sleep,
and closing his eyes he began to count sheep…"*

Based on the true story of a fox that once fell asleep in the author's garden ☺

"…truly a book for reading aloud again, and again, and again."
Louise Jordan, The Writers' Advice Centre for Children's Books

The full rhyming story is included in both editions.

Order together and let the children copy the colours!

17608142R00017

Printed in Great Britain
by Amazon